NO LAUGHING MUTTER

(A Christian Comedian's Book of
Apologies for Unkind Jokes Made under
His Breath about Others – All in the
Name of Mean-spirited Humor)

BABY CHRISTIAN

iUniverse, Inc.
Bloomington

No Laughing Mutter
A Christian Comedian's Book of Apologies for Unkind Jokes Made under His Breath about Others - All in the Name of Mean-spirited Humor

iUniverse books may be ordered through booksellers or by contacting:

iUniverse
1663 Liberty Drive
Bloomington, IN 47403
www.iuniverse.com
1-800-Authors (1-800-288-4677)

Because of the dynamic nature of the Internet, any web addresses or links contained in this book may have changed since publication and may no longer be valid. The views expressed in this work are solely those of the author and do not necessarily reflect the views of the publisher, and the publisher hereby disclaims any responsibility for them.

Any people depicted in stock imagery provided by Thinkstock are models, and such images are being used for illustrative purposes only.

Certain stock imagery © Thinkstock.

ISBN: 978-1-4759-7499-7 (sc)
ISBN: 978-1-4759-7500-0 (e)

Printed in the United States of America

iUniverse rev. date: 2/27/2013

In the dirt-polished kingdom of assassination humor, this Christian comedian was once knighted with the title, *THE GRIME REAPER...*

Hey folks! Baby Christian here...with sincerest apologies to several victims of my former warped sense of humor, for horrible things I've muttered under my breath to make friends and strangers laugh at those "unfortunate" souls I targeted – BEFORE my receipt of salvation and conversion to Christian comedy.

In time I came to discover that the only unfortunate soul was ME!!! So now I gladly submit my "I'M SORRY" list to many that I've terrorized... and to the world...

To Marlo T. of Chicago – who'd asked me to save the last dance for her at our high-school senior prom, when I thoughtlessly muttered this under my breath for friends to hear as she started to walk away...

"Are you kidding? Sweetheart, I've seen your clumsy moves! You have two left feet – both on the same leg."

LORD, NOW THAT I KNOW BETTER, HELP ME TO BE MORE KIND AND LOVING TO YOUR PRECIOUS CHILDREN. I'M SO SORRY, MARLO.

To Corbin J. of East St. Louis, IL – who began wearing hats after I said this...

"That guy's skull is so completely egg-shaped, he has to comb his hair with a Slinky."

HEAVENLY FATHER, LET ME ALWAYS REMEMBER TO SEE THE BEAUTY FOUND IN YOUR EVERY HUMAN CREATION. I PRAY YOUR FORGIVENESS, CORBIN.

To Clancie S. of San Antonio, TX – a waitress whose facial circumstance gave me an opening to sneak in this zinger...

"If her moustache were any longer, she could pull it back over her head and go trick-or-treating as Batman."

HEAVENLY MAKER OF ALL THINGS, HOW I WISH I COULD TAKE THAT GIRL AND GIVE HER A BIG HUG AND ASSURE HER THAT YOU HAVE GIVEN HER YOUR SEAL OF LOVELINESS THAT NO MAN COULD EVER HOPE TO DUPLICATE. I HUMBLY APOLOGIZE TO YOU, DEAR CLANCIE.

To Hynden W. of Panorama City, CA –
whom I used to tease relentlessly with
muttered lines like this...

"Your face is so freakishly round that when you die, your tombstone will be a rack of bowling pins."

PRECIOUS FATHER, REMIND MY HEART CONSTANTLY TO UPLIFT THOSE YOU'VE PERMITTED TO CROSS MY PATH. BLESS YOU, DEAR HYNDEN. I'M SORRY.

Be kind and compassionate to one another, tenderhearted, forgiving each other, just as in Christ God forgave you. (Ephesians 4:32)

To Zina K. of Glendale, CA – a former church member whose makeup I thought was much too thick, I made this crack...

"Once at a singles banquet, I stopped a desperate man from attacking her with a knife – because he thought she was the cake."

DEAR JESUS, CONTINUE SHOWING ME THAT MY OWN SHORTCOMINGS LEAVE ME VIRTUALLY NO ROOM TO CRITICIZE ANYONE ELSE'S. MY SINCEREST APOLOGIES, ZINA.

To Eclenzo O. of Burbank, IL – a college mate who used to preach passionately against reincarnation in favor of a Christian-defined afterlife, I once muttered this during class...

"Whew! Is that your cologne, or did your neck die and come back as a diaper?"

*LORD, ONLY WHEN I'M MINDFUL OF **YOU** CAN I TEACH MY TONGUE TO SHARE KINDNESS AND MERCY. BLESSINGS OVER YOU, ECLENZO. I PRAY YOU SHOW OTHERS THE COMPASSION I DIDN'T HAVE TO GIVE.*

To Pamela S. of Maywood, IL – whose struggle with weight was the perfect catalyst for me to say this...

"Her stomach is so flabby that when she fell on her back and the fat flew, people thought the paramedic had covered her face with a sheet."

LORD, LET ME ALWAYS REMEMBER TO TAKE INTO ACCOUNT THAT PEOPLE STRUGGLE WITH WHAT THEY PERCEIVE TO BE THEIR OWN SHORTCOMINGS – AND THAT IT'S NOT MY JOB TO MAKE THEM FEEL WORSE, BUT BETTER, BECAUSE OF YOUR UNDYING LOVE FOR THEM. PAMELA, YOU ARE A GEM IN GOD'S EYES. I'M SO SORRY I DIDN'T TELL YOU THAT.

To Ephraim S. of Midwest City, OK – a balding church deacon with a comb-over, I offered this little observation...

"His head looks like a sputtering water-sprinkler system set on freeze-frame."

LORD, I THANK YOU FOR THIS
BEAUTIFUL BROTHER WHO
HAS DEDICATED HIS SERVICE
TO YOUR CAUSE. PLEASE
FORGIVE ME, EPHRAIM.

"My command is this: Love each other as I
have loved you. (John 15:12)

17

To Anthony B. of Century City, CA – who had an extreme passion for eating, I whispered...

"The guy is such a non-stop chow hound that at the city dump, flies cover their food to prevent him from landing on it."

*DEAR FATHER, LET THIS MAN
KNOW GOOD HEALTH AND
LONG LIFE AS HE COMES
TO KNOW THE POWER
AND GOODNESS OF YOUR
EXISTENCE. I SINCERELY
APOLOGIZE TO YOU, ANTHONY.*

*Other merciless mutterings include...
to Khrystyne F. of Santa Clarita, CA – a
woman with an external-layer flesh
ailment...*

*"Her skin is so patchy that
when the economy is shaky,
she picks up part-time work as
a used tire."*

HEAVENLY FATHER, I PRAY PHYSICAL HEALING OVER YOUR WONDROUSLY MADE CHILD. BUT IF YOU CHOOSE TO LET HER REMAIN IN HER CURRENT STATE TO SUIT YOUR PURPOSE, PLEASE REMIND HER SPIRIT HOW GLORIOUSLY IT CAN SHINE BECAUSE YOU FASHIONED IT. PLEASE PARDON MY RUDENESS, KHRYSTYNE.

To Ashland A. – A severe athlete's foot sufferer whom I used to work with at a movie studio in Hollywood...

"His feet are so smelly that when he removed his shoes to powder his toes, a skunk harassed him for a business card."

*KIND MASTER, HELP ME
TO KEEP MY MOUTH
SHUT WHEN IT COMES TO
GOSSIPING ABOUT OTHER
PEOPLE'S PROBLEMS...AND TO
SPOTLIGHT ONLY THE GOOD
THINGS ABOUT MY FELLOW
MAN. THANK YOU ASHLAND,
FOR BEING PATIENT WITH
ME WHILE SHOWING ME THE
ROPES. PLEASE EXCUSE MY
OFFENSIVE BEHAVIOR.*

To Dootson D. of OKC – a man abnormally stressed over this thing called living...

"His shirts are so heavily saturated with nervous sweat, aging goldfish dream of the day they can retire under his armpits."

LORD, IF I'D ONLY HAD THE SPIRITUAL SENSE AT THE TIME TO TELL THAT POOR MAN HIS WORRIES ARE NEEDLESS, AS LONG AS HE ILLUMINATES THE DARKNESS WITH GODLY DEVOTION. I'M PRAYING FOR YOU, DOOTSON. AND I'M DETERMINED TO TRACK YOU DOWN TO BEG YOUR FORGIVENESS.

We who are strong ought to bear with the failings of the weak and not to please ourselves. Each of us should please his neighbor for his good, to build him up. (Romans 15:1, 2)

To Trish R. of Stone Mountain, GA – on her deep concern over the appearance of her lower extremities...

"Her legs have so many varicose veins, she once hypnotized a road map."

TRISH, I'M SAD FOR THE HORRIBLE CRACKS I MADE TO OTHERS AT YOUR EXPENSE – BOTH UNDER MY BREATH AND IN BLARING TONES. MAY YOU BE BLESSED BY GOD WITH GOOD HEALTH AND LONG LIFE. I'M SORRY FOR ANY PAIN I'VE CAUSED.

To Templer B. of East Chicago, IN – a young woman having to schedule regular sessions with a dermatologist...

"With that rectangular head and those puffy spotted cheeks, she looks like a barbell with acne."

WHATEVER IS BORN OF
YOUR AMAZING HANDS,
PRECIOUS SAVIOR, IS
OF A SUPERNATURAL
CRAFTSMANSHIP WHOSE
UNIQUE BEAUTY IS LIKE NONE
OTHER. MY SORROW FOR THE
HURT I BROUGHT YOU SEARS
MY HEART TREMENDOUSLY,
TEMPLER.

To Croughton V. of Lakenheath, England – a UNITED KINGDOM hero in competitive cycling, who has a fiercely uncontrollable facial tic that I commented on, when my travel buddies and I observed one of his practice runs on a London service road...

"His face is so twitchy that every time he rides his bicycle towards opposing traffic, motorists yell for him to make up his mind about which turn signal he's using."

HEAVENLY CREATOR, AS YOUR LOVE AND MIGHT STRETCHES ACROSS THE UNIVERSE, MY REGRET STRETCHES ACROSS THE INTERCONTINENTAL WATERS TO ONE OF YOUR BELOVED. BLESS THAT BRAVE WARRIOR IN HIS EFFORTS TO TACKLE HIS APPOINTED SPORTS CHALLENGES – AND EVERYDAY LIFE. YOU HAVE MY MOST HEARTFELT APOLOGIES, CROUGHTON...AND MY ADMIRATION.

*To Angela W. of Aurora, IL – a woman
who preached to all who'd listen
that weight loss was going to be her
birthday gift to herself...*

**"Her thighs are so plump that
in exercise class, she strangled
herself squatting."**

WONDERFUL SAVIOR, HERE'S ANOTHER DEAR LADY THAT FELL VICTIM TO MY POISONOUS VERBIAGE. ANGELA, I'VE SEEN ALL YOU'VE BEEN BLESSED WITH TO OFFER THIS WORLD – AND IT'S GOING TO MAKE A DIFFERENCE FOR THE KINGDOM. I ENTREAT YOUR FORGIVENESS.

Do not let any unwholesome talk come out of your mouths, but only what is helpful for building others up according to their needs, that it may benefit those who listen. (Ephesians 4:29)

To Autumn J. of Mesa Arizona – a lovely female whose modeling career couldn't take off because of a slight facial deformity...

"Her lips are so puckered that she didn't smoke cigarettes, she sharpened them."

*IN THE GOOD NAME OF
OUR LORD AND SAVIOR, LET
HIS PEACE AND JOY BE THE
BEAUTY THAT MODELS YOUR
HEART, SOUL, MIND AND
SPIRIT, AUTUMN. NOT ONLY
DO I SEEK YOUR PARDON
FOR MY OFFENSE, BUT I TELL
YOU IN TRUTH THAT YOU ARE
GORGEOUS!*

To Ted B. of South Chicago's Brainerd District – a man who gave me chills whenever he entered the room...

"His eyes are so gruesomely close together that instead of the lenses in his bifocal frames being side-by-side, they're one behind the other."

*FATHER GOD, I THANK YOU
FOR THE PROPSPEROUS LIFE
YOU HAVE GIVEN THIS MAN
SINCE I LAST SAW HIM. I
HEAR HE CREDITS YOU FOR
ALL GOOD THINGS IN HIS LIFE
AND BEARS GRUDGES AGAINST
NO ONE WHO EVER PUT HIM
DOWN. I APOLOGIZE ANYWAY,
TED, AND AM GRATEFUL
THAT PEOPLE LIKE YOU ARE
ON EARTH WORKING IN THE
SERVICE OF OUR LORD AND
SAVIOR, JESUS CHRIST.*

To Maysedra A. of Wichita Falls, TX – a lady who, in my past opinion, shared something in common with the male species...

"Her voice is so deep that even with laryngitis, she can produce an echo underwater."

I WOULD LOVE TO AGAIN HEAR THE BEAUTY IN YOUR WORDS AS YOU SPEAK OF THE FATHER'S LOVE FOR HIS EARTHLY CHILDREN. FORGIVE ME, MAYSEDRA. AND KEEP HERALDING THE GOOD NEWS!!!

To Meechy D. of Hanover Park, IL – a senior citizen whose physical appearance is weathered with a lengthy existence...

"That geezer's skin is so rubbery, his flesh attracts unrolled newspapers."

MR. B., YOU WERE ABSOLUTELY RIGHT THAT LONGEVITY IS A GIFT FROM OUR SAVIOR, AND THAT PEOPLE WHO FEAR AGING ARE THE SAME PEOPLE WHO FEAR LIVING. YOUR YEARS HAVE IMPARTED MUCH KNOWLEDGE UNTO YOU — AND I APOLOGIZE NOT JUST FOR MY CHILDISH BEHAVIOR, BUT FOR NOT HAVING TAKEN FULL ADVANTAGE OF YOUR GOD-GIVEN WISDOM.

Do to others as you would have them do to you. (Luke 6:31)

To Laurel O. of Crete, IL – who, as a former high-school classmate, had to continue wearing clothes she'd long ago outgrown due to tough economic times...

"Her clothes are so tight-fitting, nudists are offended."

*LORD, DRESS THIS WOMAN
WITH YOUR UNDYING MERCY
AND GOODNESS. MAY
SHE KNOW GOOD HEALTH,
PROSPERITY AND PEACE THAT
COMES FROM ABIDING IN THE
GLOW OF YOUR GRACE. I'M
TRULY SORRY FOR ANY HURT
I'VE CAUSE YOU, LAUREL.*

To Carlyn Y. of Mound Bayou, MS – a woman whose sturdy physique served as fodder for my acid tongue...

"She's so big-boned that an archaeologist produced a birth certificate – in which her mother's signature was the footprint of a dinosaur."

FAILING TO SEE THE BEAUTY IN ALL THE LORD CREATES IS AMONG THE MOST TRAGIC SITUATIONS OF A SPIRITUALLY BLIND SOUL. FORGIVE ME, CARLYN. I NOW SEE WHAT YOUR MAKER ENVISIONED WHEN HE MADE YOU UNIQUELY. PLEASE KNOW HOW TERRIBLY SORRY I AM.

To my own dear cousin, Jonathan Q. of Evergreen Park, IL – a trim young man I should've been protecting all those years ago, instead of muttering things in his presence like...

"The kid is so puny, a vest I thought he was wearing turned out to be his rib cage."

*JONATHAN, I AM SO SORRY
AND TRULY REPENT OF THIS
AND MY OTHER CRUELTIES
TOWARD YOU. I AM SO
PROUD OF YOU. YOU'RE A
WONDERFUL PERSON AND I
PRAY GOD'S ABSOLUTE BEST
FOR YOUR LIFE. WITH YOUR
LOVE FOR TRAVEL – AND
THAT INTERESTING FRIEND
OF YOURS WITH THE FUNNY
HAT - - THERE REALLY SHOULD
BE SOME KIND OF TV SHOW
ABOUT YOUR ADVENTUROUS
SPIRIT. I LOVE YOU, LITTLE
COUSIN - VERY MUCH!!!*

To Syndy N. of San Fernando, CA – yet another female victim of my spiritually myopic observations...

"Her nose is so wide that when she hears loud gunshots in movies, she covers her ears with her nostrils."

SYNDY, THERE IS NOTHING WRONG WITH YOUR NOSE THAT WASN'T CORRECTED AS SOON AS GOD ADJUSTED MY SPIRITUAL VISION! I PRAY ENDLESS BLESSINGS OVER YOUR SUCCESS IN ACHIEVING THAT HEARTFELT GOAL OF BE-COMING A VETERINARIAN. IN RETURN, I HOPE YOU CAN OF-FER ME A SPOONFUL OF FOR-GIVENESS.

Each of you should look not only to your own interests, but also to the interests of others. (Philippians 2:4)

To Viveca L. of Chicagoland's Beverly Hills District – a woman who developed a fear of crossing the street after suffering minor injuries inflicted by a texting motorcyclist...

"Her knee caps are so scratched, nightclub DJs hire her to sit on a spinning turntable."

HEAVENLY HEALER, I PRAY
YOU REMOVE THE FEAR FROM
THIS WOMAN AND LET HER
BE COMPLETELY LIBERATED
IN YOUR PROTECTIVE LOVE.
FORGIVE ME PLEASE, VIVECA.

And finally, to my dear friend, joke-writer and author FAULT DIZZNEY, I apologize for muttering the following five comments about you on a crowded elevator - before you made such a huge impression on me in becoming my cherished Christian brother...

1. *"That chin of his is so pointy, he can shave his neck while wearing a straitjacket."*

2. *"His face has so many lines and wrinkles that when he sheds tears, they flow sideways."*

3. *"His eyesight is so poor that when the electricity went out, he was the only one who couldn't see the darkness."*

4. *"His feet are so big that when he leaves the house and walks to his mailbox, he comes right back in tracking mud from other planets."*

5. "He's so hopelessly obese that even when he's dieting nonstop, reduced weight makes him look fat."

THANK YOU, FAULT, FOR BEING ABLE TO SEE RIGHT THROUGH MY CRUEL CRITICISMS OF YOU AND OTHERS, AND INTO MY OWN INNER PAIN AND INSECURITIES THAT ONLY THE SAVIOR COULD HEAL. FROM ONE CHRISTIAN COMEDIAN TO ANOTHER, YOUR BRILLIANCE FOR HUMOR IS ONLY ECLIPSED BY YOUR KINDNESS AND PATIENCE THAT HELPED ME FIND JESUS. YOU'VE ALREADY ACCEPTED MY APOLOGY. BUT I OFFER IT AGAIN FOR PUBLIC RECORD. BE BLESSED, DEAR BROTHER!!!

Be devoted to one another in brotherly love. Honor one another above yourselves. (Romans 12:10)

REPEN ***t****ERTAINMENT COMING FROM*

THURD/WIRM

MEDIA EUGENICS

I N   M E M O R I A M . . .

THE

SYLVIA MITCHELL

HOMEGOING

October 28, 1938 – August 20, 2012

AUNTIE, OUR FAMILY SO LOVES AND MISSES
YOU. WE CAN'T WAIT TO BE WITH YOU
AGAIN...AT THE SPECTACULAR FAMILY
GATHERING CHRIST OUR KING IS PLANNING
FOR WE WHO LOVE AND ADORE HIM.
SOON, SUGE. VERY SOON.

YOU WANT HIM...YOU GOT HIM!!!

Book Chicago's own nuttiest Christian comedian/author *BABY CHRISTIAN*, to appear at your church-related event at *info@thurd-wirm.com* or phone (818) 288-2901. Chicago's own? Uh, okay...but he's been living in Southern California for almost 20 years. And he hasn't lived in his Illinois-home state for nearly 30 years. Chicago no longer owns him. They're not even interested in renting him. Maybe if he had better table manners. Whoever heard of a person being invited to the Mayor's Banquet and bringing a doggie bag to the table – with a hungry doggie in it?

www.thurd-wirm.com

ALSO FROM

THURD/WIRM MEDIA EUGENICS...

PHRASE and WORSHIP *by Baby Christian*

THEY MAY LAUGH AT MY FLAWS BUT... *by Fault Dizzney*

MYLES A. HEDD *by The Man From A.N.K.L.E.*

Visit our comedy-loaded website for Christ-followers at www.thurd-wirm.com

EPILOGUE

Now I realize that it's one thing to poke a little harmless fun at friends and family – as long as you're also willing to poke fun at yourself – to keep all things fair. But it's something completely different to brutalize a person for attributes you perceive as "inferior" and worthy of cruel sport to entertain others.

God created us and loves us deeply. In His word, He tells us amazingly that those who love and worship Him are only a LITTLE lower than the angels!!! Christ says those who worship Him will do greater things on Earth than HE did!!! In my book, these attributes of his modern disciples are the POLAR OPPOSITES of inferiority. YOU, as a follower of JESUS, are supreme royalty! With that information, the next time we meet, let's laugh and point at other believers out of complete joy for our glorious destinies – and love our neighbors as ourselves!!!

--Baby Christian

A

THURD/WIRM

MEDIA EUGENICS RELEASE